Where Is Coco Going?

WHERE IS COCO GOING?

by Sloane Tanen

photographs by Stefan Hagen

BLOOMSBURY
CHILDREN'S
BOOKS

First published in Great Britain in 2004 by Bloomsbury Publishing Plc
38 Soho Square, London, W1D 3HB

First published in America in 2004 by
Bloomsbury USA Children's Books

Text copyright © Sloane Tanen 2004
Photographs copyright © Stefan Hagen 2004
The moral rights of the author and photographer have been asserted

A CIP catalogue record of this book is available from the British Library

ISBN 0 7475 7476 6

Printed and bound in Hong Kong/China

1 3 5 7 9 10 8 6 4 2

All papers used by Bloomsbury Publishing are natural, recyclable products made from wood grown
in well-managed forests. The manufacturing processes conform to the environmental regulations of the country of origin.

dedicated to NORMAN and CELIA KIRMAN

Where is Coco going?

In a taxi that's stuck in traffic . . .

On a train that's way too slow . . .

On a skateboard that's going faster . . .

Where is Coco going?

On a bike breezing through Paris . . .

Through the desert on a hot, hot day . . .

Passing through a scary forest...

Up in the sky enjoying the weather . . .

In a spaceship and getting closer . . .

Trains, planes, spaceships, AND a parachute???

Where **IS** Coco going?

GRANDMA'S HOUSE!!!

Acknowledgments

Grateful acknowledgment to Tracy James and Coco Nelson for all of their inspiration.
I'd also like to thank Stefan Hagen, who, once again, outdid himself with these incredible photographs.
My gratitude to Matthew Lenning for the great design, to Trudell for lending us her talents in creating the scary forest,
to Gary Oshust for his model-making skills, and to The Tiny Doll House and The Doll House Lady for always being well-stocked.
Finally, thanks to my family, and to Amy Williams, Colin Dickerman, Victoria Wells Arms, and the entire staff at Bloomsbury.
...Oh, and to Beth Altschull, for I don't know what, but she wasn't happy
about not being thanked in the last book.